For Chris, P.H.

To little misses everywhere, D.A.

First published in Great Britain in 2003 by Brimax,
an imprint of Octopus Publishing Group Ltd
2-4 Heron Quays, London E14 4JP

Mc Graw Hill **Children's Publishing**

Text copyright © Peter Harris 2003
Illustrations copyright © Octopus Publishing Group Ltd 2003

This edition published in the United States of America in 2003 by
Gingham Dog Press
an imprint of McGraw-Hill Children's Publishing,
a Division of The McGraw-Hill Companies
8787 Orion Place
Columbus, Ohio 43240-4027

www.MHkids.com

Library of Congress Cataloging-in-Publication Data is on file with the publisher.

Printed in China.

1-57768-437-0

1 2 3 4 5 6 7 8 9 10 BRI 09 08 07 06 05 04 03 02

The **McGraw-Hill** Companies

Perfect Prudence

Illustrated by
Deborah
Allwright

By
Peter Harris

GINGHAM DOG
P R E S S

Columbus, Ohio

Prudence was perfect at everything she did.
She was the best at multiplying and dividing.

She was tops at singing

and dancing

and acting, too.

So when the school decided to put on the play, *Jack and the Beanstalk,* the teachers all agreed she'd make a *wonderful* Jack

and a *magnificent* Jack's mother

and a *sensational* both ends of the cow

and even a *tremendous* giant.

Cast List
Jack
Mother
Giant
Cow front
Cow behind

And guess who they thought would be terrific at doing the lighting, raising the curtain, and making the CRASH sound when the giant fell off the beanstalk?

All this didn't leave much room for the other children in the play. Just Karen Brown playing her banjo.

But since Prudence could play it better than Karen could anyway, this soon changed to Prudence playing Karen Brown's banjo.

Didn't the other kids get fed up with Prudence being allowed to have all the fun? Well, they were used to it. The teachers were always saying that if a thing was worth doing, Prudence was the only one worth doing it.

As for Prudence, she never disagreed with her teachers.

The school hall was packed on the big night.
Everybody had come to see the famous Prudence.
A producer had even flown in from Hollywood.
The teachers were nervous. Would Prudence pull it off?

But Prudence wasn't scared. She knew she'd be a hit. She was already imagining what it would be like to sign autographs and to live in Hollywood.

Then the moment came. Prudence dimmed the lights, tuned up Karen Brown's banjo, walked onto the stage, and gave the performance of her life.

As Jack, she would have brought tears to your eyes when she sold the cow.

As the cow, she would have had you tapping your feet when it danced a jig.

As Jack's mother, she would have had you
singing along to her duet with Jack.
(Prudence was also a talented ventriloquist.)

As the giant, she would have had you hiding
under your seat when she shouted . . .

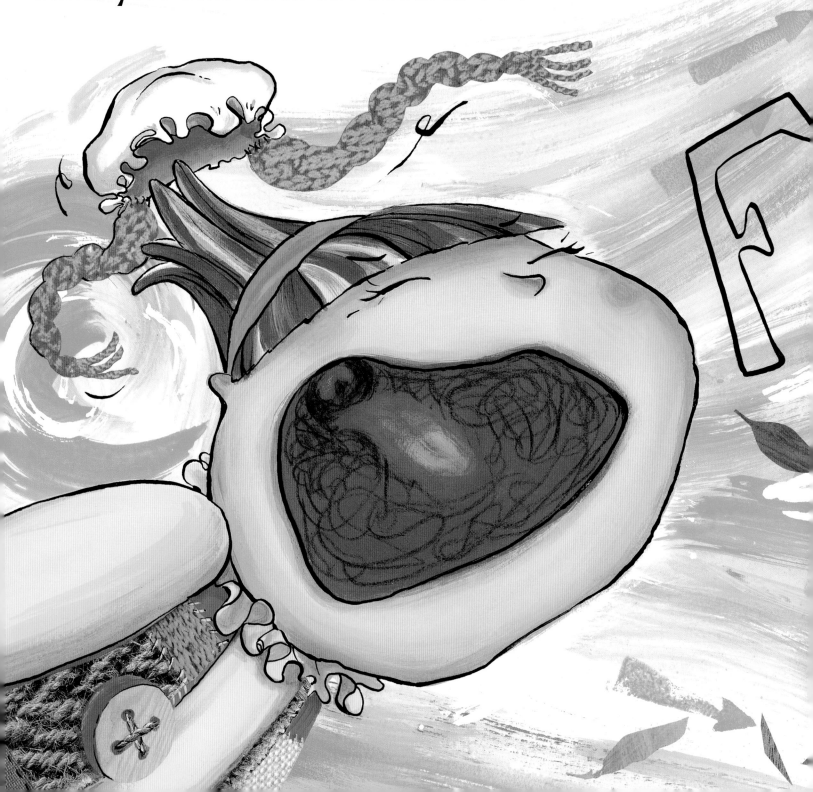

Yes, you would have done all those things. If only Prudence hadn't been so busy playing all the parts

and doing the lighting and making the **CRASH** sound when the giant fell . . .

. . . that she'd forgotten
to raise the curtain
in the first place!